Published 2015 by Geddes & Grosset, an imprint of The Gresham
Publishing Company Ltd, Academy Park, Building 4000,
Gower Street, Glasgow, G51 1PR, Scotland

Reprinted 2018

Copyright © 1997 The Gresham Publishing Company Ltd

All rights reserved. No part of this publication may be reproduced,
stored in a retrieval system or transmitted in any form or by
any means, electronic, mechanical, photocopying, recording or
otherwise, without the prior permission of the copyright holder.

Conditions of Sale:
This book is sold with the condition that it will not, by way of trade
or otherwise, be resold, hired out, lent, or otherwise distributed or
circulated in any form or style of binding or cover other than that
in which it is published and without the same conditions being
imposed on the subsequent purchaser.

Written by Judy Hamilton.
Artwork by Mimi Everett, courtesy of Simon Girling & Associates,
Hadleigh, Suffolk.

ISBN 978-1-910680-53-7

Printed and bound in Malaysia

3 4 5 6 7 8 9 10

Susie & Sam Visit the Dentist

Geddes & Grosset

Susie and Sam were in the bathroom, brushing their teeth. Dad was helping.

"Make sure you brush the teeth at the back of your mouth," he said. "Clean the top and the bottom."

Susie and Sam carefully brushed all round and then Dad brushed their teeth as well, just to make sure. Dad and Mum always helped them to brush their teeth, but today they were taking extra care, because they were going to visit Mrs Green, the dentist. Susie and Sam went to see her twice a year, once in summer and once in winter, to make sure that they were looking after their teeth and gums properly.

In the waiting room at the dentist's surgery, the walls were covered with posters. "Healthy teeth, healthy gums", said one. "Avoid decay, brush twice a day", said another. The posters all had pictures of teeth: teeth in smiling mouths, sparkling teeth, sore teeth full of fillings and holes and tiny teeth poking through babies' gums.

Mrs Green popped her head round the waiting room door.

"Ready, Susie and Sam?" she said. Susie and Sam followed her into the surgery. Dad came too.

"Who's going first?" said Mrs Green.

"Me," said Susie, climbing up onto the chair, "Sam went first last time."

"Right, Susie," said Mrs Green, "let me have a look at your teeth."

She pushed a button by her side and the chair tipped right back.

"Oh!" said Susie. "You've got a new picture on the ceiling!"

"Something nice for you to look at while I am looking in your mouth," said Mrs Green. "Now, open wide please!"

Susie opened her mouth wide. Mrs Green picked up a little silver mirror with a long handle. She used it to help her to look all around Susie's mouth. She gently touched around Susie's teeth with a shiny metal instrument.

"No holes," said Mrs Green. "You keep your teeth lovely and clean, Susie!"

Susie was very pleased.

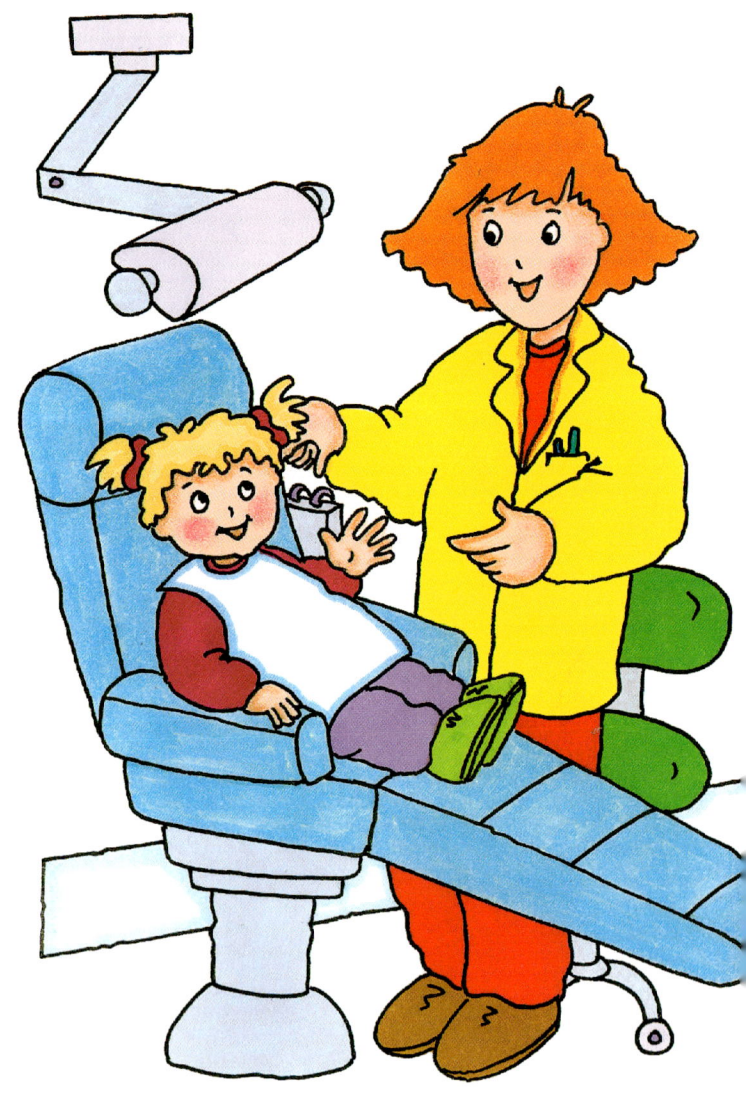

"Not too many sweets, I hope?" said Mrs Green.

Susie shook her head. She and Sam did get sweets sometimes, but only for a treat. Dad and Mum knew that sugar is very bad for your teeth.

"One of your top teeth is a little bit wobbly," said Mrs Green. "It will fall out soon to make room for a new adult tooth. You'll have to look after your adult teeth extra carefully, won't you?"

"I know," said Susie. "Dad told me. Once all our adult teeth have grown in, we don't get any more new ones. And if you get a hole in your tooth it hurts."

"Yes," said Mrs Green. "We can put a filling in the hole to mend the tooth, but it's better not to get a hole in it at all."

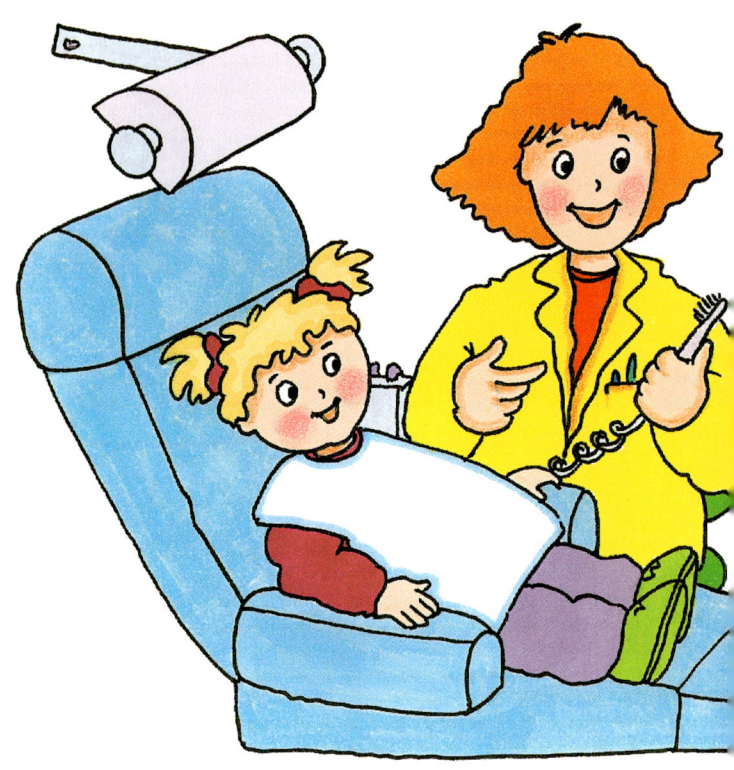

"Grandpa's got false teeth," said Sam. "He didn't go to the dentist when he was a boy and his teeth got so sore that he had to have them all taken out. I don't want that to happen. I'm going to look after my teeth."

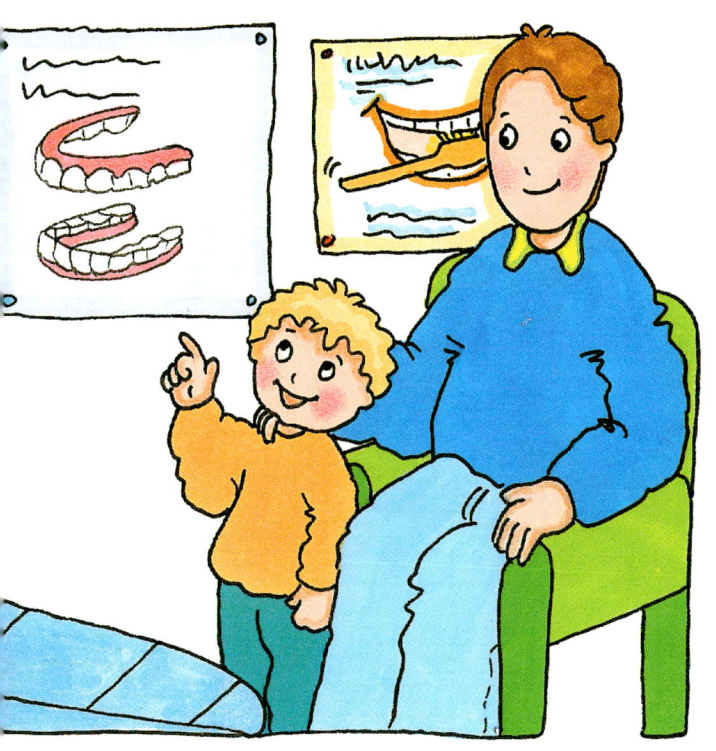

"I'm glad to hear it," said Mrs Green. She took another instrument out. It was attached to the machinery by the side of the chair.

"Do you remember this, Susie?" she said. "It's my electric toothbrush."

Susie and Sam liked the electric toothbrush. The pink toothpaste which Mrs Green used tasted nice and the toothbrush tickled! Mrs Green switched it on and gave Susie's teeth a good polish. She squirted a little water into Susie's mouth to rinse it. Then she used another instrument from her machine to suck out the toothpastey water.

"That's just like a little hoover," said Sam, who watched carefully.

"It is indeed," smiled Mrs Green. "Now, Sam, it's your turn!"

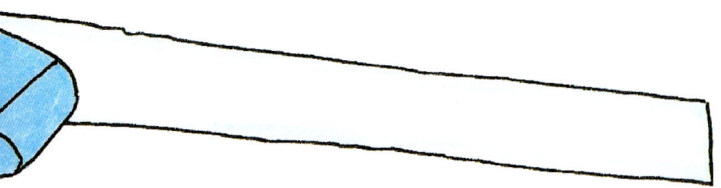

Mrs Green inspected Sam's teeth and cleaned them with the tickly toothbrush.

"Top marks, Sam!" said Mrs Green.
"Perfect teeth, just like Susie's."

Dad was very proud of Susie and Sam.

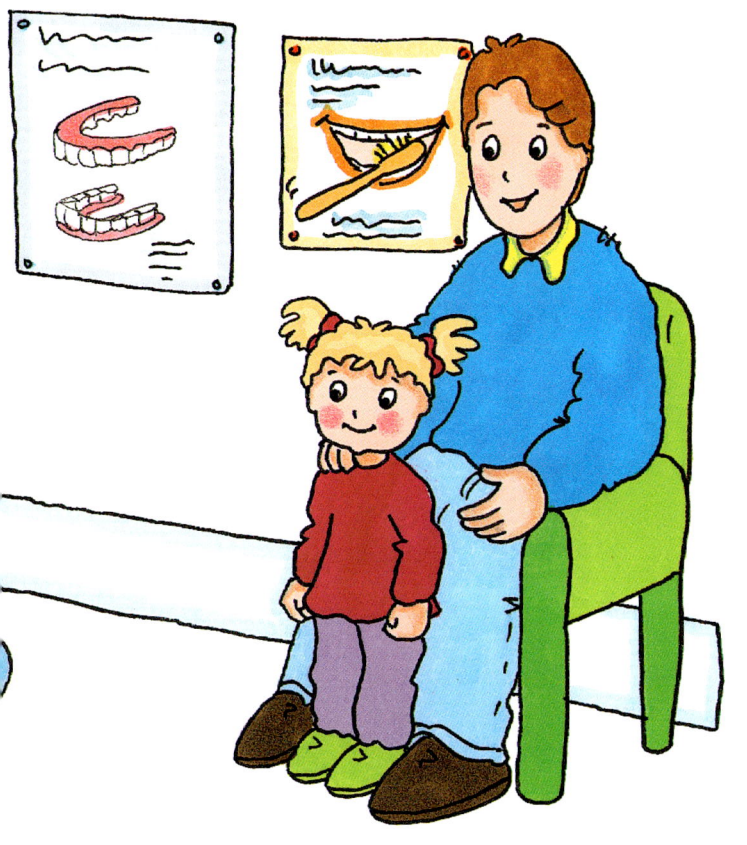

They said thank you to Mrs Green before they went home.

"See you in six months' time, and keep up the good work!" she said.

On the way home, Susie began to fiddle with her wobbly tooth.

"Why are you doing that?" asked Sam.

"I'm going to put this tooth under my pillow when it comes out," said Susie, "and see if the tooth fairy will come."

Sam tried to wiggle his top teeth, but nothing was loose yet. He would have to wait a little longer for a visit from the tooth fairy.

"I think I'll be a dentist when I grow up," he said. "Then I could have a tickly toothbrush, just like Mrs Green."

"Good idea," said Dad, with a smile.